ORLAND PARK PUBLIC LIBRARY

3 1315 00161 4879

P9-CME-004

APR   1993

DISCARD

ORLAND PARK PUBLIC LIBRARY
AILEEN S. ANDREW MEMORIAL
14760 PARK LANE
ORLAND PARK, ILLINOIS   60462
349-8138

DEMCO

Emily Arnold McCully

SCHOOL

Harper & Row, Publishers

ORLAND PARK PUBLIC LIBRARY

School

Copyright © 1987 by Emily Arnold McCully
Printed in the U.S.A. All rights reserved.
Designed by Bettina Rossner.
3 4 5 6 7 8 9 10

Library of Congress Cataloging-in-Publication Data
McCully, Emily Arnold.
  School.
  Summary: A curious little mouse decides to find out
what school is all about.
  [1. Mice—Fiction.   2. Schools—Fiction.
3. Stories without words]   I. Title.
PZ7.M478415Sc 1987   [E]   87-156
ISBN 0-06-024132-2
ISBN 0-06-024133-0 (lib. bdg.)

For Harriet

1614879

ORLAND PARK PUBLIC LIBRARY

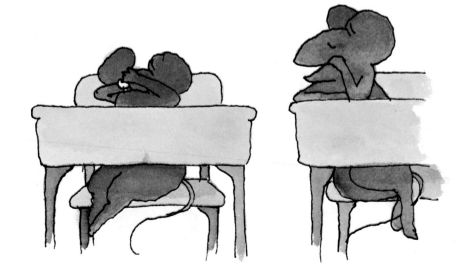

ORLAND PARK PUBLIC LIBRARY